Thick As A Brick

Little Book of Pain #2

Craig Brownlie

Please find trigger warnings at the back of the book.

***

Everything for Suzanne and Aaron

With gratitude to Ken B., Adam H., Heidi S., Candace N., Tim M., Laura G., Don. N., Derek C., Brian K. & Terry E.

Ron R., Scott C., and John Z.: you're remembered in these words

CONTENTS

THE COEFFICIENT OF DRAG

I am the green potato chip
Left behind in the bag

I am the last conscript
The one who sags

I am the one who is skipped
In time
For I lag

I dangle on the edge of lips
Out of mind
No zig
   only zag

I unbalance the ship

Cut the line and embarrass the flag

I am not worth the trip
Unmarked by sign and unburdened by swag

I am the bottom of the pyramid
Wide of hip
Barren of sunshine
Identified by toe tag

Thick As A Brick

"Rhea!" Nick yelled at his wife.

Lifting the cardboard box at her feet, she leaned backwards and bumped into the six-foot newspaper stack behind her. Their son, Carter, stood in the hoarder-made cavern on the other side of the pile. He groaned under the tabloid avalanche.

Later, the ER doctor told them Carter had a displaced fracture in his left forearm.

The next day, Nick woke to his mother calling at 7 a.m. "How's Carter? Are you at the hospital?"

"Fine and no. He has a badly broken arm." Nick dressed while he talked. Carter's twin sister, Monica, would be awake soon. Almost thirteen, she did not have the decency to sleep late. "It's Sunday, you know. I could have slept a little longer."

"You should have called me."

"You live four hours away, Mom. I would have later."

"I spoke to Dominick last night and he feels terrible."

He should have felt terrible about accumulating so much crap. "Carter will be all right."

"I'm sorry I asked you to go out there and help him. When he told me the sheriff had been by and warned him something had to be done, he sounded so broken."

Nick's mother and her cousin Dominick remained the only ones left in their generation. They had not been particularly close until Dominick's father died. Now the two of them talked every week. "It's all right, Mom. We made a start. Honestly, Dominick doesn't seem interested in cleaning house."

Once Dominick held back all four of them. Every bundle they grabbed had to go through a full inspection before they hauled it to the curb.

"I really do appreciate your helping. I know Dominick does too."

"We did what we could..."

"I told him he shouldn't expect you there today, but you'd be back Saturday."

"I'd love to, Mom, but the kids have baseball on Saturday and..."

"You're not going to tell me Carter is going to be out on the baseball field when he broke his arm?"

Nick breathed deeply and warned himself not to let her get to him. "I'll see what I can arrange."

Nick's grandmother had moved off the family farm in a fit of pique at the age of eighteen. The property passed to her younger brother. Neither family branch prospered, but they coped in different ways. Nick's branch had been tight with money and lived sparse lifestyles. They used what they had. When they finished with something, they disposed of it. Dominick's branch saw no reason to dispose of anything. Dominick proved to be the last in a line of hoarders.

"His father tried to repair the state of things out there. You should have known Dominick's dad better. As a young man, he played music like you. Bring Carter back with you next week. It'll do him good to overcome any fears he may have of those newspaper stacks."

***

On Saturday afternoon, Dominick caught Nick heading out the back door bearing a box of old sheet music.

"What do you want with all this?" Nick jiggled the box, upsetting the piles inside. "You don't even play the flute, do you?"

"Not the point," Dominick gripped cardboard and tugged. "I need to know what's going."

Nick had no idea why he had to examine everything. If he had not opened the box recently, then what did it matter now?

Dominick tipped the flaps open on the box and stirred the contents with his forefinger. "It can go. Unless you want it. You teach music, right?"

"I teach high school music, and this would cause allergy attacks in half my class." Nick headed outside. They had purchased extra garbage barrels at the Home Depot. He dumped the sheet music into one and crushed cardboard into the recycling.

Not emotionally able to go right back inside, he walked along the road a few paces and then down the old dirt path to the ruined barn. The old family farm had not been a going concern in his mother's lifetime. The barn had a partial roof and no way to reach the remnants of the second floor.

Nick considered the broken timber of the barn, the peeling paint on the house, and the desolate fields beyond them both. Things fall apart. Nothing ever holds.

Walking past the barn he leaned on a solitary fence post. Once, his ancestors needed to demarcate their fields, but they mismanaged them. He took a few steps and felt hard crunching underfoot which signified the weird geography of western New York. Between the strange outcroppings of Chimney Bluffs and the ancient growth of Bergen Swamp, the earth beneath your feet combined deep time and unexpected geology.

Near his shoes, the dirt glistened in the sun. Crouching, Nick saw black shards knitted into the earth. No wonder nothing grew here. They had turned their planting area into a glass dump. He made a mental note to ask if the family ever owned a bottling company. More than one thing had happened to take the family from prosperous farmers to a lonely hoarder in a couple generations.

Inside the house, Nick found his cousin rummaging.

"Here it is," declared Dominick, his pleasure rising like a word balloon above him.

Nick looked over his stooped shoulders and saw an open box holding two dark mugs and a bag of black dust. "Is that the same stuff from out back? Where did the glass come from?"

"My father made the glass," muttered Dom. He raised the mug and it sparkled in afternoon sunlight.

"So, they did have a small factory on the property."

"Not a factory." Dominick's wattle rattled as he protested. "A kiln."

"Is that how the barn burned down?"

"Doesn't matter," explained Dominick. "The important thing is we have the powder." Brandishing his find, he brushed past Nick.

We are so finished cleaning up this mess, thought Nick, as he followed. They found Carter using his one good hand to page through old Sunday funnies from the *Democrat and Chronicle*.

"I like Prince Valiant," commented Dominick as he stood over the boy. "Nice hair, good story."

"Yea," agreed Carter, scratching at his cast.

Dominick put down his bag on a convenient magazine mound and sat beside Carter. Nick watched their eyes move in unison as they read. He recognized a good time to transport another load outside.

He could sneak a pile out the back door, so Nick headed to the basement which contained the oldest layers. The old paper smell hung like a haze. Nick grabbed as large a bundle of yellowed periodicals as he could manage and stumbled as they crumbled in his arms. Quietly, he emptied a nearby bin of old cans and dumped the magazines into it. Skipping the creaky step as he walked upstairs, Nick exhaled when he stepped outside. Quickly he moved around the house and returned with the empty bin.

On his fourth trip, Nick stopped at the sound of his son gagging. Carter rasped as Nick rushed into the front room. Dominick stood in front of him, nervously shuffling and shaking his hands. Carter looked pained, but alive and breathing. On the table in front of him, one of the black mugs lay on its side, its contents spilled across the funnies, dissolving the paper into primary color blobs.

Nick dabbed at the mess with his fingertip. "What the hell is this?"

Carter heaved twice.

Dominick retrieved a glass.

"Water? With nothing in it?" demanded Nick.

Dominick nervously edged around him, nodded, and handed it to Carter. They all waited while Carter drank tentatively at first and then a bit more. He coughed clearly and indicated he could breathe.

"What did you do?" Nick studied the old man's face, head half melted into his chest as age overtook the body.

"I... wanted to fix what had happened. The powder fixes people sometimes." Dominick folded the mess on the table and carried it into the kitchen.

"Are you okay?" Nick crouched in front of his son, shielding their conversation. "Be careful what you accept around here. I know he's family, but he doesn't make good decisions."

Carter sipped more water and agreed vigorously.

Nick found Dominick at the kitchen counter going through index cards. "These are your great-grandmother's recipes."

Dominick proffered one called black hole tea, amounting to hot water and crushed powder collected from the fields.

"Is this the one you made for Carter?" Then he saw the bag of black dust on the countertop. "I have no words." He tossed the card into the air and walked out of the kitchen.

"Carter!" he called when he found the parlor empty. "We're going home, now." He heard a faint call from upstairs. Nick had not set foot in the bedrooms in years.

He had been little, and Dominick brought him upstairs to see his models. Nick needed a companion during the semi-annual family meals. The two of them would sneak away during the lull before dessert. They went to Dominick's bedroom, and he would pull the drapes. He sat at the desk and Nick would perch on the edge of the bed. They counted down together from ten and then Dominick switched off the lights. The ceiling burst into a beautiful glow-in-the-dark map of the night sky. Dominick taught Nick the constellations and he had been so proud when Nick named them all in one go.

Nick knew they needed to go home. He needed time to deescalate Rhea about this powder incident. Walking up the stairs, he wondered at his ability to accept such a thing.

Nick found his son in Dominick's bedroom, the lights out, and the ceiling manifested in all its glory. Seated beneath such splendor, Nick felt transported out of the house. He could not align the disorder in the other rooms with the glory overhead.

"What did you say, dad?" asked Carter.

Nick replayed the last minute in his head, "It's not real."

"For paint and stickers though...," Carter liked the scene well enough. "What's over there?" The boy tilted his head, looking out of the corner of his eye beyond Sagittarius.

An emptiness hung on the ceiling past the constellation. Without thinking, Nick walked toward it. "The center of the galaxy." Someone had found a paint darker than desolation and marked this spot. Enticed, Nick reached out. Time loosened its hold and Nick felt existence fall aside. His head ached like a migraine experienced vicariously.

The lights in the room flashed on. Carter stood beside the switch. Looking back at the ceiling, Nick could no longer identify the barren location. He extended his hand to see if the paint felt different anywhere. Turning back to his son, Nick resisted running across the room and hugging him. Something lingered in Nick's mind making him afraid of and for the boy.

"What's this, dad?" asked Carter, pointing at a telescope by the window.

"A Stargazer. When we came here for meals, if the adults took too long with dessert, then Dominick would let me use it to look at the stars."

"Do you think he'd mind?" Carter pointed at the eyepiece.

"It's daylight. You aren't going to see anything." Nick moved to the door and headed down the stairs. "Don't try to learn astronomy from Dominick. He has different names and stories which will confuse you when you talk to your friends or teachers."

They found Dominick on the back porch, his arms crossed, a sullen expression on his face.

"I tried to help the boy," he said soon as the screen door closed.

"I know, but you shouldn't hurt him in the process."

"You'll see," responded Dominick.

Nick put his hand on his son's shoulder and guided him to the car. "Maybe we'll be back next week." He waved. "Otherwise, we'll see you when we see you." Seated with the windows closed, he advised, "Don't accept food from Dominick without running it past Mom or me. I'm sure you'll be fine, but enough with Dominick's experiments."

"It didn't taste bad, only crunchy."

***

On the following weekend, Rhea and Monica joined Nick and Carter to continue the debriding project. Dominick had uncovered another box of comic books and sat with Carter on the back porch going through them. Nick wanted to show Rhea the fallow field and the shattered barn. Monica tagged along.

"Now we know why the farm failed," said Nick, tugging a chunk of smooth opaque rock out of the dirt. "My mom said things fell apart, but she never knew why."

"They must have done well enough," said Rhea. "You usually had Thanksgiving dinner and stuff out here, so how bad could it be?"

"They always had a scheme or three going: goat farming or renting out space to church groups or even selling rocks."

Monica shaded her eyes and scanned the horizon. "It goes on pretty far."

"I don't know how much is still in the family."

"Grandma has a picture of somebody winning a prize at a fair with a giant pumpkin," continued Monica. "Did it come from this field?"

"I remember the picture! It showed my uncle, standing out here. The gourd took five men to move."

"Did they eat the seeds after?" Monica asked.

"I don't think the seeds or anything inside are very good when they grow so big," answered Rhea.

Nick added, "Those seeds could not be eaten. The pumpkin split open before the end of the fair. Inside they found a bunch of black rocks, probably like these. They accused him of cheating, but nobody could figure out how. I think he opened another business selling the rocks to farmers who wanted to do their own experiments and win their local fair."

"We ought to head back." Rhea tugged on his sleeve.

Nick shrugged.

Dominick and Carter had left the back porch, though the box of comics remained. Rhea found them in the kitchen. "What's been going on here? What have you done now?"

Nick rushed in to find Dominick and Carter seated at the table, before them an old Dremel tool and Carter's cast split in two. "What the hell?"

"I'm all healed!" Carter waved his hand around, flexing the fingers. "Dom thought so and we decided to take off the cast." When he saw the expressions on his parents' faces, he added, "His idea."

Dominick ran his fingers over the black pattern beneath the boy's skin. "It's good with broken bones. Not so good with indigestion or headaches, but it fixes some things. I learned from my Mom and Dad." He met their eyes. "I felt bad when Rhea injured Carter."

The pattern shifted into exotic shapes which disappeared from memory even as new figures formed. Then, all of it faded to the shade of pale skin.

Nick stepped away from his son, until he stood in the next room. If he had not, then he might have grabbed a knife off the counter and cut the boy's arm off.

***

Three nights later, when Nick walked into their bedroom, Rhea asked, "What have you there?"

"My old Walkman. Carter has been listening to CDs on it instead of going to sleep. Can you believe he likes Jethro Tull?" He took out a bottle of aspirin, poured out four, chewed them into powder, and swallowed. He needed to erase the images which floated before his eyes: taking a knife to Carter's arm;

standing in a field naked playing a flute; and watching his life contract into a small black marble.

"I don't think you take those right," commented Rhea.

"They're pulverized enough."

"You've been taking them like candy ever since you Carter came home without his cast." Rhea muted the Colbert show. "I don't want Carter and Monica going out there again."

Nick wanted to watch the show, so he agreed, "Makes sense."

"You're not listening to me. Carter had nightmares this week before the cast was cut off and I don't mean normal wake up and have a drink in the bathroom stuff. He cried out on Thursday night."

"I don't remember."

"Of course, you don't. You sleep through the garbage trucks every week. Maybe it had something to do with the cast or something at school. What about the powder Dominick gave Carter?"

"It's out of his system now." Nick reached for the remote.

"His arm works well enough." Rhea moved the remote away. "Check him in the morning. I think little bits of stuff are coming through the skin."

"Fine, I'll call my Mom and say we're done with Dominick."

"You can't. You need to find out more about what that crazy old man gave to our son."

Nick studied her face. "Okay." She finally looked ready to surrender the remote. He needed to numb his mind.

***

When Nick walked into the house on the next Saturday, Dominick asked, "Where is everybody?"

"I'm here!" Nick had practiced his response in the car.

Dominick levered himself out of his chair, "Come with me." He ambled to the basement stairs and descended. "I know you have questions. Your mother called. You might not believe this, but your mother can be very rude."

"I might," Nick smiled.

The old man shifted from side to side as they wound through two lanes of boxes. "When you disposed of those old papers a couple weeks ago, you didn't search very hard. If you had tried to remove what I am about to show you, then we would have had words."

And then I probably would have stopped bothering to help here, you old nutjob, thought Nick. Maybe we can still have words today and I won't have to feel any guilt about leaving you and your hoard to the sheriff. "What in the world?" Nick pulled up short.

"This is what I wanted you to see." Dominick stood before shelves of canning jars containing desiccated fruits or sticks or maybe dried snakes or possibly old pipes.

Nick picked up a jar and examined the contents. When Dominick did not object, Nick studied a dozen before he pronounced his opinion. "Are they old broken-down flutes?"

"Father tried all of them. When they didn't work, he broke them into pieces. He saved them because he wanted a record of his experiments."

"But why? What did he do with them?" Each jar held one flute, most metal, but some wooden. Most looked like beginner school instruments. Some had been hand-carved and a few of those bore folk symbols. The curved glass distorted the instruments inside as well as his fingers wrapped around the jars. "My hands..." The jar shattered on the basement floor.

They considered the chaos at their feet until Nick said, "I forgot whose hand held it." He wanted to break more of the jars. He wanted to hear additional crackling, high-pitched noise.

After kicking the mess toward the wall, Dominick nodded and picked up another of the jars. "See, there, the extra holes. Grandpa altered the flutes. He cut them and poked them. If you look closely, I think he stepped on some of them and dropped weights on them."

"So, he liked to play broken musical instruments? He didn't do it where anyone could hear him, did he?"

"He used to do presentations at local libraries."

Nick did not know how to respond, so he returned the jar in his hands gently to its place on the shelf. He nodded as though trying to calm a slightly crazy dog.

Dominick suddenly shifted containers to nearby surfaces by the armful. "Some families break because of money or lies." From closer to the wall, Dominick pulled out the now empty shelves revealing wooden file cabinets. He tugged on their brass handles. Opened, they revealed a neat arrangement of old notebooks, scrapbooks, and folders.

"Your mother never had interest in the past. She gave you a skewed idea of what caused the family rift. Your grandmother probably told her a bunch of stories about moving out and your mother never wanted to hear otherwise. Your grandmother left my father behind to deal with everything." Dominick gestured at the surrounding mess, acknowledging it as a burden.

Unsurprised by his mother's unwillingness to delve into the family history buried in this damp basement, Nick asked, "Can we bring the chests upstairs?"

They hauled two containers to the kitchen and placed them on the floor. Then, they stood and contemplated the implacable documentation imploring their attention.

"Our relatives never imagined our branches would be standing here like this."

Nick had to agree. "It's late and I'm tired." He bent to lift one of the chests.

"You're not...," Dominick protested. "I want all of it brought back in exactly the same order next Saturday."

"Help me put it in the car and you have a deal." They even shook hands before Nick drove away.

***

"'Order can be brought to bear on the chaos.' 'A great shard must have been cleft from the black hole.'"

Rhea stopped him there. "You've been reading to me for two nights. It's not making more sense as you go on. What are you hoping to find?"

"I had to argue with Dominick for these two crates." Nick sat on the sofa with two thirds of a box piled on the coffee table. The rest had been returned to the wooden chest in a close approximation of the original order. "Maybe I thought something valuable hid inside, like a rare nugget of reason. Some of these letters look like they're from important people. I hoped it would explain what happened to my grandmother and her brother. The farm must have been nice once."

"You can't fix the past."

"Maybe I can understand it." Spreading old letters on the table resonated like walking through dried leaves. "He contacted all these universities from around the world. He tried astronomy departments and geology. He heard back from quite a few. This one guy in New England, a retired professor at Miskatonic University, seemed particularly interested. He studied a sample of the dust and confirmed it as extraterrestrial, part of the primordial fabric of the universe. Dominick's grandfather knew it wasn't from this planet since he had watched it fall from the sky."

"Then where did the crystals come from."

"The dust fell on May 29, 1953. By the end of June, they'd lost everything—the crops, the animals."

"Why did the people survive?" Rhea asked.

"Because they stayed inside when it fell?" He dug around in the chest. "Here's something he had the local vet write to the bank, probably to justify late payment on the mortgage. The vet says he examined the deceased livestock. On autopsy, their insides had dissolved or imploded. Whatever had killed them had done so from the inside. He goes on to say not to blame the family even if he could not explain it completely." He looked at Rhea with dawning concern.

She said, "Basically, they had this toxic waste fall from the sky and wipe out their livelihood." Rhea contemplated her feet for a few moments. "This would be the same shit your cousin fed to our son?"

Nick recognized the conversational minefield. He nodded in resignation. After carefully rebuilding his piles, he placed everything back inside the wooden chest. "I'm going to go practice a little before bed." He grabbed his ever-present aspirin bottle and tried to remember when he last took some. He shrugged and devoured four.

"Wait."

Nick had almost made it to the stairs.

Rhea stopped him, "What does music have to do with all this?"

"What do you mean? I haven't come across anything in the papers."

"The Miskatonic professor suggested something about activating the dust with sound. He has these weird drawings. You said something about all those broken instruments."

"The old man lost his mind when he lost his fortune." He went back to the pair of boxes. "Nothing in the first one." He unlatched the second and pulled out a few random selections. "More correspondence. Maybe you're right." He held out some pages to Rhea.

"My family watched *Cosmos*," Rhea said while scanning. "This looks like a black hole. He had terrible handwriting, but doesn't it look like 'aural activation' and 'implode'? Could they have made the livestock explode or implode or die or disintegrate?"

Nick nodded, "Which made the farm dangerous. Here's some stuff about how to make dynamite inert. This is another letter from Miskatonic talking about what a stable form of the powder might look like."

"Like those damn crystals scattered all over out there. Maybe if we dig them up, then it can become a viable farm again or be sold even." Rhea stopped reading and grabbed Nick's arm. "You practiced last week and then Carter felt better."

"I don't remember... He was better at Dominick's, but..."

Rhea held his gaze, "No, before then, but it never occurred to us to remove his cast. Your crazy cousin thought to do it."

"I did play the flute some," Nick looked pained. "Have you seen my Walkman? I took it away from Carter last week, I think. Did he take it back?"

Nick and Rhea felt the pull toward their children before the world collapsed.

Monica screamed upstairs.

They ran until they no longer could. The hallway leading to Carter's bedroom elongated. Monica stood in her open doorway. Rhea reached her first. Nick stopped when he saw the paint draining out of the walls. The carpet turned to darkness, not the absence of light, but the departure of being. Balanced on one foot, Nick saw only abyss where he meant to step.

"Carter!" Nick yelled. He stretched forward, trying to grab Rhea. She enveloped Monica, protecting her from whatever awaited them as the end of the hall edged closer. She hugged their daughter tightly, leaving no free hand to grasp Nick. He watched them turn pale, then gray, then they disappeared.

Nick's fingertips burned, and he pulled his hand inward, forcing his feet to propel him backwards at the same time. He landed on the carpet, facing an expanding void.

Like wallpaper peeling, the sky appeared before him. Then the tree in the neighbor's yard displayed in full color. Nick exhaled and realized his hearing returned as though poured into his ears. This felt no different than a night sitting on his back porch except he sat on the floor inside his house. His home ended less than a yard in front of him. For an eternity, the world did not respond and then the sirens drew near.

***

The first police car to arrive found Nick probing the opening with a golf club wrong way round. After they had coaxed him a safe distance away, they called civil engineers and safety officers and the gas company and the Red Cross. They locked him in the back of a patrol car.

The authorities searched for debris without success. No one could explain how a third of a house evaporated any more than they could see the bottom of the small cavity in the earth, no wider than an inch or two, where the basement ought to be. Everyone who investigated had to be pulled away from the deep, dark hole to nowhere.

When they next checked on him, Nick had grown unresponsive. He finished the night in the psychiatric ward.

***

The house looked like a giant monster had taken a bite out of it, thought Nick. Someone had covered the exposed rooms with plastic tarps to prevent further damage. He stood on the sidewalk. Neighbors came out of their homes. A couple waved, but Nick only stared back at them. The guy next door shouted that they had kept an eye on the place for him.

He had grown accustomed to feeling numb, needed the deadness of sensation.

No one at the hospital had advice other than he needed to grieve. None of them could believe his story. Still, they discharged him as soon as his insurance ran out. Nick had checked into the Motel 6 by the highway, but he wanted to see the house.

He saw the forearm in the grass and ran. The black dust moved about on it like the last time Nick saw the body part attached to his son. About three yards from the limb, he slid on the wet grass to a halt. Slowly, as he approached, he realized his mistake—a stick covered in ants. Their mandibles cleaned something organic which Nick turned away from.

An emptiness in his stomach made him take the long walk up the driveway and go inside. He could see the humor in using a key to unlock the door with gaping holes only a few yards away. Humor looked interesting from his detachment.

Inside, he smelled the mildew brought about by the elements. The kitchen stank from bad onions and unfortunate growths in the refrigerator. He dragged everything out to the trash barrels. Perhaps he could have fought the force which destroyed his family if their home had held more gravitas—more weight—more junk. Perhaps Dominick had responded reasonably to an unbelievable power by building the only defense imaginable.

His excuse for heading home had been his need for clean clothes. On the second floor, looking through rips in the tarpaulin, the terrible night rushed in and filled the spaces in his mind. As his eyes focused, the light of the stars elongated for an eternal moment.

"Fuck it," he muttered and turned for downstairs and the front door. The wooden chests by the sofa remained exactly as he had left them.

He considered his next actions for minutes containing more than sixty seconds. Celestial bodies danced in his vision, stretching out like fingernails dragged along his nerves, setting sparks racing before his eyes as he lost consciousness.

***

Nick lay on the floor. His limbs twitched from their scatter-shot layout until he could sit upright. Everything in the room remained in place, even the wooden chests. Crawling slowly, he settled on the floor beside the first box.

When his world collapsed, Nick sat here with Rhea and worked on a mystery. Now, he had anger pressed tight in his chest, nursed by those lonely nights in the sanitarium. He would make his rage grow into a worthy sacrifice to any god who would return him to his family.

***

His mother called. "Where are you?"

"At the house." He could hear her searching for a response. "Is it a mess?"

"Somebody covered over the holes. Our neighbors have been keeping an eye on the place."

"Be careful people don't spend your money on something not worth saving." She sighed. "I don't know how you remain so placid about all this. Your family..."

"I know what happened to my family."

"You need to find some peace and a way to live."

"How are you okay with this?" Nick demanded.

"Who's okay?" she shouted into the phone. She continued at a more measured volume, "Our family is cursed ever since the damn dust fell from the sky. I couldn't cope with it by yammering on about it or displacing it into some nutty hoarding. I carried on. You breed and you outlive the curse generation by generation."

"Didn't work out," muttered Nick. "I'm going back out to Dominick's."

"I never should have roped you into helping him."

He disconnected because regrets were for people who misunderstood time.

***

Nick parked in front of the old country house. Abruptly, he sat in his hallway again watching his family and his world dissipate. Now it sparkled—then laser lines—finally his life circled the drain before sinking into a dreadful abyss.

He found his bottle of aspirin in the glove compartment and chewed a handful. The paste proved too much to swallow, and he spit as he made his way to the front door.

Not bothering to knock, Nick walked inside. Dominick sat at the kitchen table and nodded a greeting. "I wondered when they'd let you out."

"I want my family back." Nick pulled out a chair and sat. "I have the wooden chests in the trunk."

"I want to help." Dominick tugged the loose skin on his neck. "Your mother knows better, you know? She acts like I started all this, but she knows it happened where our families intersect. We embraced the chaos and made it into an anchor. My grandparents—your great-grandparents—died soon after your grandmother deserted her family. Maybe you can understand now…"

Nick had no time for recriminations. "I teach music to kids because sometimes it makes their brains work a little bit better. I do this to support my family. Now I don't have a family and I think it's because of what happened here. You've read all the shit in those chests. Let's put a pin in the philosophy of hoarding for another time and maybe fix our family a little."

"I bet you're wishing you hadn't thrown out all my Dad's music."

***

The sun sent tentacles of light over the eastern horizon. Nick stood in the backyard. Dominick had helped drag a card table into the fields behind the house. On it, they placed a selection of flutes from the basement. Nick drove to a local school band supplier and made a deal on a dozen others. Then he raided the cabinets at his school and grabbed four more, including a piccolo. They modified them all per instructions gleaned from their reading.

Dominick sat under a blanket in a nearby lawn chair. "Try the tiny one first," he encouraged.

Nick thought he could use techniques outlined in his reading. Mix the trove of information in the chests with Stephen Hawking, and anything felt possible. He would experiment where he could only hurt Dominick and himself. Once he understood the forces in play, then he would go home and set things right.

He grasped the piccolo and played a scale before tentatively launching into a holiday carol. The notes reached high enough to slice molecules. Searching the sheet music in local shops had not uncovered anything better than pop tunes, soundtracks, and musical hits. Little felt appropriate for bringing order to chaos. He switched to *Tubular Bells*.

Nothing happened...

He considered the tiny flute in his hand. They had not mangled it. Inspired by the contents of the Mason jars, they had altered the other flutes. Nick tossed the metal cylinder in Dominick's direction and tried another flute.

Nothing happened.

He selected a bent flute. He twisted another as he blew across it. He tried numerous selections.

Nothing happened!

The sun rose as Nick worked through all the flutes. Most sounded horrendous or produced no sound. His head ached. He would buy a dog whistle and a baritone flute once the stores opened.

Then, Dominick stood over him, offering a hand. "You collapsed. It's not easy playing the flute, especially damaged ones."

***

Later, at the kitchen table, Nick drank cola and chewed aspirin. He studied the Miskatonic correspondence and ignored an urge to sort again the entire contents of this horrid house. He had retrieved the remaining chests from the basement. They contained sheet music and outlandish designs for musical instruments, covered in despondent comments about their failures.

One cabinet held clippings from newspapers and magazines, but no journal articles. These provided a history of meteor showers and plain oddness falling from the sky: amphibians, humongous hailstones, and so much more. Pride of place had been given to a carefully tied folder of newspaper articles.

Khulna, Bangladesh, was the most recent location among the press clippings, a decade after the dust landed on the farm. After World War II, Arequipa, Peru, suffered through a similar downpour, according to American missionaries in the area. The only other location documented was Marrakesh, Morocco, in 1924. Calculations and theories covered the interior of the folder. No pattern emerged.

An article from *Fate* magazine compared these incidents to wormhole manifestations. The author claimed to have visited those sites and personally documented subsequent destruction, always foreshadowed by an absence of matter, including air, according to eyewitnesses. Dominick's father had saved multiple copies of the article because he had written it.

Nick had found comfort in this desperate, rotten house over the last day. The insanity which had devastated his family could only be met with the same madness. He turned to see Dominick standing across the room.

Nick's frustration boiled over, "If these mountains of crap had crushed you first, then they wouldn't have buried my family."

Dominick desultorily washed dishes at the kitchen sink.

Nick needed space and went to the front room where he organized cardboard boxes into level piles. Opening the first one, he found a stash of old record albums: Traffic, Canned Heat, Genesis, and, of course, Jethro Tull. Somebody had a thing for rock from the Sixties and Seventies. Dominick seemed the right age.

"Looking to see if they're worth anything?" Dominick asked from the doorway. "Probably not enough to pay a hauler."

"Not yours?"

"No way. Punk music for me, you know."

"They all featured flute players."

"These belonged to my dad." Dominick fiddled with a Genesis album.

"When Carter discovered my collection, I had a lot of this stuff."

Dominick nodded and led Nick out to the barn, which had a fruit cellar. Standing at the top of the dirt steps, Nick thought how the farm had been littered with stashes of junk. The smell of soil and roots rose from the pit cut in from the side of the barn ruins.

"The powder did not destroy the barn. Neither did the kiln," said Dominick as they descended. "This did."

Nailed against the wall, a goat-man effigy hung in tatters. Broken bits of old skin hung from a cacophony of bones. The skull dangled precariously, observing everything in the small room.

"The creepiness on the wall occurred to my father from his reading. It's supposed to represent some sort of cosmic flute player. Another attempt by my Dad to save us all."

The empty eye sockets of the monstrosity held Nick. Notes blown through an alien flute on a scale unheard on Earth entered Nick's mind.

"My dad thought he could eliminate the dust or coalesce it and end this horror." Dominick pointed at a wooden table. "Before he died, he bought outdoor speakers and wired them up to this stereo system. Most people used the same model speakers to play music by an outdoor pool."

Nick ignored the effigy's stare and studied the audio equipment. The components looked well past their sell-by dates. "Maybe the speakers still work. Any idea where they are in the fields?"

***

They had connected a used CD player through fresh components to the speaker wires sticking out of the dirt wall over the fruit cellar worktable. He had barely slept since checking out of the psychiatric hospital. Nick made sure Dominick kept pace by plying him with caffeinated drinks.

Nick insisted they try a used 98 Degrees CD first, not wanting to tempt the gods of order or chaos. He had combed two different record stores to fulfill their needs in classic flute rock and inoffensive pop. The latter provided the control for their experiment. Soon, the fields erupted with *I Do*.

"All right," said Nick as he emerged aboveground. Refusing tears, he screamed at the sky, startling Dominick. "Why don't you mark the speakers with those stakes we bought?" Before turning and heading for the farmhouse, he watched Dominick amble into the field.

The hot work in the fruit cellar made him need the bathroom and a cold drink. When he returned, Dominick stood in the approximate center of the speakers, immersed in boy band music. Nick had brought bottles of Coke from the fridge, and they clinked glass. Nick watched his fizz settle down before sipping. Then he headed for the sound system. "Enough of this love-is-grand crap." He stopped at the top of the steps and looked at Dominick. "I'm going to play with the volume. Let me know if it grows too loud for the neighbors."

"The neighbors aren't going to notice," commented Dominick though Nick had already gone below.

The boy band stopped singing. The speakers buzzed with a sudden jump to very loud. Ian Anderson sang and then the flute break came.

Dominick grabbed at a heaving pain in his stomach. He shook the soda bottle. Sediment floated through the beverage, like dark stars in oblivion. "You could have given me a choice!" Then he imploded.

Nick had run to the surface to watch. A great absence pulled and pushed him in a confusion of physics. His perception evaporated in a moment lasting forever.

***

Awake later, Nick studied the crater left behind by Dominick and decided it did not look like the remnants of a wormhole, but he could hope. After struggling upright, he retrieved the compact discs from the fruit cellar and went out to his car.

Nick's rudimentary understanding of astrophysics gave him hope. He drove home after stopping at Best Buy. The cashier eyed him suspiciously in his mucky clothes and desperate demeanor but sold him their largest portable stereo without comment. At the post office, he mailed an envelope containing some black powder and an explanation to Miskatonic University.

Nick tore the tarps off the gaping maw of his home before trudging inside and mounting the steps to the second floor. He topped off a fresh bottle of cola with black powder from the bag in his pocket. The carrier at his feet held the empty bottle from his drive home.

He sipped at the soda. He chugged through his gag reflex.

Nick had carried only one CD in from the car. The last thing he heard-- Ian Anderson singing "wise men don't know how it feels to be thick as a brick."

I Accidentally Erased Your Message

I accidentally erased your message
That sound of your voice, rhythm of your text
All gone from the record with no vestige

Our relationship had no other moorage
Adrift without backup, without context
I accidentally erased your message

But also gone is waterlogged baggage
Now left without ruts, not anchored, not vexed
All gone from the record with no vestige

We ought to dry our tears and acknowledge
The past is past, and the future comes next

I inadvertently lost your message

If we let slips of the finger ravage
Then love no more has reason or pretext
All gone from the record with no vestige

Leaving me to free memory storage
That our brief time together had annexed
I accidentally erased your message
All gone from the record with no vestige

The Circus Came To Town

"Grant, how are you?"

"Sitting down to dinner, Norm, and all set for tomorrow. Looking forward to it."

"About that. I'm calling to say you don't really have to come in."

The conversation paused like it had since Grant had decided to return to work after the death of his wife. The two of them waited to see who would lob the next phrase.

Norm tossed, "We're still seeing a lot of attention from the local news. Sally what's-her-name called-- the reporter for News9 asking whether you'd be back tomorrow. They clearly want to ambush you."

"Slow news week, right?" Grant wanted to confront Sally on camera and tell her to stop trying to paint him into a corner. He had done that well enough all by himself.

"Honestly, Grant, I think they like the local angle on a national story. You took a stand and people are fascinated by it."

"Like when they slow down at a traffic accident..."

***

The post office at Coleville was its most notable feature ever since I80 passed twenty miles north while crossing Pennsylvania. In the last half century, the highway exits up in Barnum had blossomed chain restaurants and the nearest supermarket.

Grant Piece inherited the house across from the Coleville PO before he had married and started raising a son. The wraparound porch held enough chairs for the three of them and a guest. Louise had been after him for years to replace the ceramic table stained with coffee circles. Early on, it felt too heavy with its iron legs but now he read its surface like tree rings.

The lack of traffic meant Grant could sit on his porch and consume his caffeine and watch his son, Ben, play basketball in the driveway before taking him to school in the morning. Even when Ben was younger, they did not have a fence across the front yard.

With Barnum CSD Middle School on remote learning due to the coronavirus, Grant did not want to drive into work. The local phone company made a big deal about how they increased upload and download speed to facilitate working and studying over the internet, but they skipped boosting the signal for Coleville. Grant signed in before sunrise so he would be offline before Ben needed to attend his first class.

As he sat on the porch sipping his coffee, Grant studied the future hard. He liked his old routine of dropping off his son, stopping at Wawa, and then going into the tiny office building down the road from Barnum. He used to drive into Manhattan every quarter, but management cancelled those visits. Two months into the pandemic, even the Zoom meetings tapered off to a trickle. His boss sent feedback by email, often in the middle of the night. He always delivered his work on time.

When the trailer trucks appeared over the hill on Route 43, Grant put his cup down, appreciating the solid clunk of it on his favorite table. Stepping off the porch into the front yard, Grant saw the small convoy contained seven or eight vehicles. They slowed in front of his house to the point Grant thought they might ask him for directions.

They pulled into the church parking lot across the street. Your Servants' Church of St. Peregrine Laziosi had been closed for a decade, though Stan Weissberg held the keys for the diocese. Grant had last been inside for Louise's memorial service.

Soon as the third truck passed, Grant took seriously the words painted on their sides. The circus had come to town. This felt like an unfortunate miscalculation on their part. The Green Banana Travelling Circus and Educational Petting Zoo must be utterly lost, which had to have taken some effort in the age of Google maps.

The last truck slowed before making the turn. The passenger leaned out the window and considered Grant. "Good afternoon!" The gaunt face bore a goatee accentuating his recessed cheeks. "I hope you're planning to stop by this evening. We're in town for one night only!"

"What are you doing here?" Grant wondered.

"What? Why, we're here to bring a little sparkle and share a little mystery." His smile bisected his face. "Tell your friends and acquaintances, enemies and annoyances to plan now for the only show in town! One night only!"

The truck pulled into the parking lot across the street. Grant admitted they had no competition.

***

While Ben did the dishes after supper, Grant monitored developments at St. Peregrine. The trucks had formed a circle and stretched a big top over the space in the center. A ticket booth appeared closer to the street with no indication of admission price or hours. Grant mulled over asking Ben if he wanted to cross the road and check it out. Instead, he dozed.

***

Sandra Lynn pulled her Ford Focus onto his front lawn. She tugged herself free of the driver's seat and waved to Grant, "I hope you don't mind, but it looks like the circus has filled up the church lot!" She wore the same pants suit she wore as a guidance counselor at the high school. Walking across the grass to Grant, she carried a Tupperware container. "I thought maybe this would cover the price of a parking space. It's tollhouse cookies like the recipe says on the package."

Grant allowed she could park on the grass for free if she wanted though he accepted the cookies. He asked her to wait a minute while he stepped inside and retrieved Sandra's pan which previously contained a lasagna. "Ben and I appreciate all the food everyone's brought by..."

Sandra took her cookware back and nodded, "We're all so sorry about Louise, her being the first one so sick in the county and all."

"Sandy, you know she might have been the first person to die in the county, but not the first case, right?" Grant regretted the outburst as soon as the consternation appeared on Sandy's face. Louise often reminded him they had chosen this as their home. "I'm sorry, Sandy." He suspected his face did not look apologetic.

She stepped closer. "No one blames you for what happened to Louise. You be sure to share some of those cookies with Ben." Sandra started to walk away.

"Sandra, where did you hear about the circus?"

She dug around in her purse and pulled out her phone, "I thought everyone in the area got a text." She took a couple more steps and turned again, "I know when I lost Herb that I struggled to accept it as the way it had to be." Sandra did not wait for a response before moving for the ticket booth across the street.

Grant bit his tongue and went inside. Damn right, Sandy, nobody should blame him. Chance and insanity had more to do with it.

He tore his cell phone off the charger. He could barely read the words as his hand shook. Sure enough, he had a text: "When the CIRCUS COMES TO TOWN no one wants to miss out! ONE NIGHT ONLY! ST PEREGRINE'S from sunset until no one's left! Say password FALCON at the gate for a free facemask!"

As Grant came down the stairs, Ben emerged from the kitchen, "Can we go to the circus? It's across the street." Then his son saw his face. "Dad?"

Lately, Grant's face contracted into a topographic map of pain and anger whenever he sat still for more than five minutes. For months, his relationship with his son relied on excuses and explanations. Their home echoed with Louise. "Did you receive a text also? How's the homework situation?"

"I finished it before we ate."

"Bring your phone in case we separate. And a jacket." Grant turned away.

Ben reappeared with his jacket. "Is it safe to go?"

Grant considered saying no, but he needed to be somewhere with people. He could not stay at home, picking up food in parking lots and shopping online forever.

"You better believe it." When he saw Ben wince a little, he added, "We're going to wear masks and so will everyone else. If we see anyone without one, then we'll come right home. It's only across the street. Besides, we're immune, aren't we?"

"They said online the vaccine doesn't last forever."

Grant placed his hand on his son's shoulder and nudged him toward the door. When they reached the edge of their yard, Grant extracted a wrinkled mask from his pocket and donned it. Ben followed his lead. Grant counted about twenty cars lining the sides of the road. As they crossed to the church, another one slowed and parked.

The overhead sign bore pictures of clowns in facemasks while accentuating the creepy and hiding the cheery.

"How much?" asked Grant at the ticket booth.

The elderly woman exhaled smoke from her cigarette before repositioning her mask. The inside of the plastic-glass had tinted yellow. She slid a wooden block from the small aperture for passing money and tickets, letting fumes escape, and causing Grant to step back. "Look who's scared of a little smoke," smiled the woman, punctuating her sarcasm with a hacking cough. Her mask dropped below her nose with the outburst.

"Over the nose is how it goes," said Ben.

"What's he saying?" demanded the ticket seller. Without waiting for an answer, she added, "He's adorable. Two greenbacks for him and ten dollars for you."

Ben stepped closer to the booth and declared, "Falcon!"

The old woman watched every move Grant made as he extracted the cash from his wallet. After he paid, she waited to hand him the tickets until Grant repeated "Falcon." She passed him two masks with their stubs.

Walking away, the bright lights shone beneath the makeshift tent. Passing between two trucks, signs promoted the entertainment, including the usual carnival games and sideshow acts. A wooden circle marked out a small ring in the center. Inside the ring, a clown dressed as a sad doctor wore a sandwich board declaring the space off-limits to any "non-essential non-circus entities." The clown gestured children closer. He leaned over the barricade and listened to their hearts with a giant stethoscope.

Grant shied away from the clusters dotting the midway. Overhead spots created pools of light within the dark gray and Grant stuck to the dimness. Not ready for public conversation, he avoided encounters with people he knew.

Ben nudged him toward the nearest wagon which bore a hand painted sign: "CuRiOsItIeS" in different colors for each letter. Grant hesitated, looking for a ticket taker. No one stood by the open entryway. Grant wondered how they managed with so few workers.

Inside the wagon, management had marked a one-way path weaving past various exhibits. The first held an old desktop computer. The screen kept flipping upward every few seconds, so it took a moment to understand the display, which looked like an archaic version of Facebook. Ben studied everything while Grant moved ahead. Ben's questions about the taxidermized Chupacabra caused Grant to bring up Wikipedia on his phone. They moved quickly past the dismantled medical ventilator.

They admired a miniature Ohio State stadium made from toothpicks, the nearest side a little crumbled. After the last bend, they faced a curtain with a cardboard sign pinned in the middle: "original victims of the pandemic."

Grant turned to Ben. Before his son touched the curtain, Grant tried to find a side exit. Perhaps Ben did not read the sign because he plunged ahead. Grant followed.

A dim light on their left focused on a dead animal floating in a tank. Ben asked, "What's a pangolin?" He read the name off a card.

"I don't know. It looks like an armadillo..."

"A really big one...," added Ben.

When he pushed the exit door, instead of opening, an overhead light turned on and showed a human body floating in a huge tank, his eyes sewn shut. Bits of skin muddied the water. Grant read the card taped to the glass: "courtesy of our friends in..." Someone had ripped the end of the label away.

The exit gave way. Grant felt the outside air as Ben rushed back to the midway. Ben waited near the foot of the steps, eyes wide open. "What's that smell?"

Grant took his hand instead of answering, "We're going home."

Ben held still. "What about the games? We haven't been anywhere in so long."

Grant frowned before remembering his covered mouth. He scanned their surroundings and headed for the nearest booth. Catching a whiff of fried food as they walked, his stomach trembled. He turned toward the corndogs and watched a stranger buy the treat on a stick. She tugged down her mask and took a bit before moving out of the way of the customer behind her. Ben stood as still as his father, watching as the hot dog disappeared in a rapid sequence of bites.

"Pick whatever game you like," said Grant.

Ben led them toward a racing derby. Grant steered him away as he could not face the race car selection: ambulance, hearse, ... The fishing game looked calmer and Ben shifted with Grant's tug.

"Everyone's a winner!" repeated the carney. In exchange for Grant's cash, he handed Ben a tiny plastic rod. Quickly the magnetic hook latched onto a fish. "There you go!" The booth runner pulled the fish free and popped it open to reveal a piece of paper. "What have we here? Something special from the orange bin!"

The young man bent under the counter and picked through an unseen selection. "You're too young for an off-market vaping kit, right? How about a stuffed toy? I have an armadillo-thingy and a Bob Hope dressed as a doctor. That must be a collector's item. No? That leaves candy. There are these questionable detergent pod-looking treats? No? Fine, then we need to go with these candy pills. Guaranteed to do no harm except to your teeth. Take only as directed by your parents. Now get out of here."

Father and son wandered back onto the midway in a daze. A clown stepped before them and fashioned a balloon animal. The clown mimed at Ben to indicate a desired creature. Dressed as a paramedic, the parody dragged a helium tank along bearing a stenciled "General Operatin' & Surgeryin' Hospital."

When Ben did not name an animal, the clown poked the boy in the chest with a giant plastic thermometer. Still not hearing any request, the mime lowered his facemask and asked, "Come on, kid. Do you want a dog or a sword or something?"

Ben cringed, either at the revealed mouth filled with smoker's teeth or the small crowd gathering for a show. Grant took his cue and led Ben from the talking mime. The circle of onlookers parted as he shoved through.

Then he saw Sandra walking with a teacher from the high school. Grant headed for the nearest truck, focusing all his attention on the three sullen chimpanzees caged on the flatbed. Bowls of water and food lay around their small enclosure--multiple hay bales their only offers of comfort.

One of the apes dozed, popping awake before teetering from its perch on the edge of a block. Another desultorily tugged straw loose, making two piles after examining each strand carefully. The third looked back at Grant, who turned to Ben to comment and realized his son had wandered off. Their constant proximity of the past months made this a jarring discovery. Grant gripped the bars of the cage and forced himself to allow Ben laxity in their umbilical cord.

The nearest chimp moved closer when Grant focused on him. The animal burbled its lips in a gesture dismissive and offensive. The chimpanzee came to the bars in front of Grant, who removed his hand, but did not back away. The animal's inquiring expression made Grant think of a reflection.

Then, the long, strong arm of the chimp reached out and touched Grant's face. Grant fought flinching as he remembered news stories about people injured by wild pets who had bitten them. The long hand caressed his cheek in a kind gesture. Then Grant felt a hard tug and checked for a wound. The chimp held his facemask, dangling from a long finger. The chimpanzee scampered back to his drowsy companion and aroused her with loud cries.

Grant felt his face for any wound and found none, but he could not stop shaking. He stepped back. A teenage couple stumbled into Grant's pool of light and cringed. They gave him a wide berth.

Reexamining himself for a scrape, Grant realized his lack of a facemask caused the reaction. He called after them, "The monkey took it!" This attracted more looks, all of which changed to alarm as Grant repeated the words twice more until everyone recognized the Grant Piece, the one whose wife had died from the virus. He heard the muttering.

A security guard approached. At least, it said so on his shirt. He also wore face make-up and a flamboyant orange wig.

"Would you come with me, sir?" he asked with a voice which jumped pitches every two syllables.

"Is this an act?" Grant wanted to find Ben and leave.

"Right this way, sir," the clown motioned him to a small tent labeled SeCURE-itty, the S backwards.

Grant hoped they could help locate his son. Stepping through the flap, Grant gasped at how far back the space inside went.

"Have a seat, sir. I'm sure we can straighten this all out in a moment and have you on your way."

"Is this about the mask?" said Grant. "Don't you have extras you can lend me?"

The clown sat behind a dayglo desk with oversized plastic accessories. He lifted the receiver off the bright red Edison phone, "Quick, send in the winch. This guy doesn't know how to take a seat."

Grant sat. "I don't know what you want."

The security officer brandished a large yellow notepad and green pen which he licked through his mask before taking notes. "Why did you come here without your mask?"

"The monkey took my mask," said Grant.

"So, you're hallucinating monkeys now too. That can't be good. We have apes, but no monkeys. Perhaps you saw flying monkeys? Do you have a temperature?" He checked his desk drawers and found a foot-long thermometer. "It's rectal which is fine by me but maybe not something you can get behind."

"I'm telling you about the monkey in the wagon."

The clown leaned across the desk in a pose of confidentiality. "Would you be referring to the chimpanzees? They are apes, sir, not monkeys!"

Grant stared into the heavily lined eyes and rose to his feet. "The ape took my mask!"

"Oh, so angry- sit down!"

Grant settled down. "I came in wearing a mask. They wouldn't have let me in."

"You know, the word around the midway is you're the sort of person who doesn't wear a facemask. I hear you made your wife and son..."

"That's a lie!" yelled Grant. "I didn't know... I didn't know how bad this would be. I thought we would feel a little sick and we'd be safe."

The clown extracted a huge pair of white gloves out of a pocket and pulled them on. Then he reached across the desk and took Grant's hands. "How could you have known? Am I right?"

Grant pulled back as soon as the tent flap opened. A second clown security officer walked in with Ben. "Dad!" The boy moved toward Grant, but hesitated, "Where's your...?" He pointed at his mouth.

"The chimp took it. That's his story and he's sticking to it," answered the first clown.

Ben walked to his father and reached into his pocket, withdrawing the mask they had received at the ticket booth.

Rather than put it on, Grant contemplated the cloth and string bearing the print of a large foolish grin. "How did we end up here?"

Explaining Life To A Pre-Adolescent On A Friday In September

Paging through pictures of a war

A more noble war

How do I explain the arrogance

That would venture his future

For a handful of gold

    Dick Cheney should have a ditty

    About when he was young and pretty

It's like that zombie movie from the other night

No, the other one

The one that made you laugh
Because they were so stupid and slow

It is absolutely
True that Dick
Cheney could use a limerick
Mainly because we all could

There was a bad man from Wyoming
Who tried to hide his dark side but it kept showing
He stole from his friends
And screwed most Americans
Who gave and gave and gave without knowing

I want to talk about a world
So big it can hold
Lies and hubris
And oil and avarice

Which would tear these bedroom walls away

And then it's bedtime
Time for a song
A story
And a glass of water

Writing Home from a Great Remove

July 1839

Dear Eleanor,

Ranjit Singh has died at last. He was a great man, but also more, a good one. On many occasions, I saw him exhibit a charity exceeding the generosity displayed by our Christian brethren. From my first audience with the maharajah, he assailed me with question after question. "What sort of crops do you grow?" "Do you rotate your fields?" "Do you drink wine?" "How much?" "How many wives do you have?" "How many children?" His interest never waned whether the answer was brief or long.

Ranjit Singh ruled one of the largest empires ever seen on Earth. I have it on good authority that his passing has reverberated in London, Paris, and Berlin. No doubt Saint-Petersburg has likewise taken note.

The great king surrounded himself with beauty, temporal and eternal. His childhood affliction left him much attuned to what this world can offer. Never have I seen such jewels or such exquisite specimens wearing them. Indeed, the man knew his own pleasures.

My grief intensified as the king lingered for days while we waited for his passing. Part of his most important retinue, I attend in the personal living quarters throughout the ordeal as Sikh practice demanded. In his benevolence, the emperor distributed many gifts as he faded. I carry a diamond for you near my heart as a present from his majesty.

I had hoped I would be traveling homeward to Rehoboth instead of this missive. After eight years in the Maharajah's service, I find my presence is now required by his successor. Kharak Singh is the eldest son and growing into his new role. I hope once his comfort has been attained, I can again formally request dismissal from my post overseeing the kingdom's gunpowder production.

As a senior minister to the dead king, the vizier privileged me to hold a position of honor at the funeral. In truth, I would much rather have been any other place, most especially on our plantation. How I long for the smells of our tobacco and our cotton.

You should have seen the funeral procession. A quarter mile of soldiers marching two by two cleared a path through the citizens. A golden sailboat bore the emperor's body, driven onward by the loudest noise I have ever heard. Drums and horns mixed with the wails of the mourners as the dead king passed. Next came four queens each borne upon her own golden throne.

Along with other members of the royal court, I stood at the end of the procession near the funeral pyre. As the queens neared, they removed their bracelets and other gems and tossed them into the crowd. The bearers lowered them beside the king's pyre, positioned much too close.

My surprise must have been apparent for Sohan Suri, historian and friend to the entire court, offered me assurances the four queens knew their honor and willingly participated in the ceremony. Still, my heart beat in my ears as bearers placed the royal corpse across the laps of the four queens.

Seven concubines followed the queens and stepped forward. Men of the household gathered them into a close circle beside the pyre before placing a mat over them. The mat had been soaked in oil.

The king's son and successor brought the torch forward and lit the pyre. In my last view of the queens, I beheld their clenched expressions. I know not what thoughts of grief or loss brought them to this point, but I pray to their gods and mine their memory be blessed.

As the flames rose high, two pigeons flew into the fire, much to the approving cries of the crowd. I wanted to ask Sohan if the young girls and the birds were also willing and grateful, but he had moved from my side.

Tradition required honored guests to remain at our position for the next three days while the fire burned down, and the corpse-handlers raked the ashes. Finally, they divided the ashes by some method known only to them into five piles.

Thus, the king and his queens took their final rest in marble urns.

In the hope I have not horrified you, dearest Eleanor, I wish you also to know not only how foreign these past years have been but to find reassurance I have found importance and respect so far from home. Never before and never again do I expect to offer such a vigil as this.

I find myself much aggrieved to learn of the passing of Thomas. He could be an impetuous son, too quick to anger, but I approved of his active nature. From what you wrote, I gather his management kept you affluent in my absence. I suppose you have recalled Beauregard from college, and I sincerely hope he has been a help to you.

With the assistance of our boys, you managed well those first few years after those fools in our legislature deputized me to seek trade outside our normal partners in Europe. At times, I regret following the advice of those French businessmen and embarking for Goa. You have always done credit to the household, so I am sure Beau feels well pleased upon his arrival back at Montrefuter.

Admonish William Dell for overstepping his sheriff duties. His method of avenging Thomas became much too harsh and will prove costly to us in the short and long run, though he held the proper intent. Thomas should have sought help before confronting those who spread rumors about the loss of voting rights among the field houses. Why anyone should care about a law passed four years ago, I know not. Besides, the limitation only applied to free blacks. Ours never could vote even if they claimed an opinion.

Beau's first task will be to replenish the fieldworkers at the market in Fayetteville before the next harvest. He should bring a good adviser with him since he is inexperienced. Reverend Daniels always had a good eye and appreciated the opportunity to leave the county. Also, if prices and timing are better further away, then Beau should give it good consideration. Remind Beau to obtain assurances at any auction house his new stock will last more than one season to say nothing of the journey to Montrefuter.

How I miss you, Eleanor. I cannot stand another day here, but I will because I have fresh hope of safely departing. Once accepted at his court, permission to depart proved impossible to obtain. The British have increased their pressure since the passing of the clever old king, believing they can gain the entire Punjab.

I do wonder at times how you must struggle to understand my letters. If only I had mastered a fine art and could draw you a picture of these people and their land. Believe me when I tell you it is fair for those living here, but nothing like the peace and beauty of our magnificent home.

With the deepest regard,

Charles Greene

Superintendent of H.M. Gunpowder for His Highness Kharak Singh,

Lahore, Empire of the Sikhs

Master of Montrefuter,

Rehoboth, North Carolina, United States of America

IN THE BOOTH BY THE JUKEBOX

She said she liked David Bowie
Especially this one particular song
I didn't see the connection
Because I hadn't traveled her road

We shared a pitcher of brain stompers
She punched up *Drive In Saturday* on the jukebox
That night she told me about the fair
She said the 4H Barn was like the song

Dense as I was, I sang along with her
About the training ground for rapers
She spat the misheard lyrics with venom

Filling our glasses with the last of the booze
She found me wanting

To help, to protect, to fix

She slid five dollars and four quarters on the table
She wanted another round
She wanted the song to stop

THE A-FILES

According to recently declassified A-files, one summer afternoon in 1947, itinerant preacher and civilian pilot, Kenneth Arbogast, was using his plane to search a remote area of the Cascade Mountains for proof of a foreign invasion. Scanning the ground, he banked his aircraft in a sweeping turn over the town of Mineral. Arnold saw a brilliant blue-white flash across his plane's wings. Desperately looking around, Arbogast saw a tight formation of nine "peculiar-looking babies with wings." To the north of him, they headed in his direction—very fast. He later reported: "They didn't fly like any aircraft I'd seen before. Maybe it would be best to describe their flight characteristics as being similar to a flock of geese." He was certain the United States didn't have such advanced aircraft, but what about the Soviet Union?

Kenneth Arbogast was, to all outward appearances, a pillar of society, a successful minister at a young age and an acting deputy auxiliary police officer for Wichita County, Kansas. In later years, Arbogast reported several more sightings. Whatever the truth about Arbogast's story, public interest in angels grew exponentially. Over the coming years, thousands of people have reported encounters with holy beings.

On June 28, 1948, the Air Force gave unexpected support to Arbogast by reporting that a pilot in a P-51 Mustang fighter over Lake Mead in Nevada saw five or six glowing objects hovering in the sky. According to official military memos, the glow came from "tail-lights or halos."

The Fifties and Sixties saw Americans moving beyond mere sightings into direct contact with angels. In the ensuing decades, reports have taken a more sinister turn.

The adumbration phenomenon is an umbrella term used to describe a number of assertions that angelic creatures kidnap individuals. Many such encounters are described as transformative or pleasant, but others called them terrifying or even humiliating. Reports of angelic contact have been made from around the world and throughout history.

Alleged abductions are usually closely connected to apparition reports, and are reportedly conducted by inaptly-named cherubim: short, pale-skinned humanoids with large heads and enormous, dark eyes (to say nothing of the requisite wings and halos). It is possible that some "abductees" may be unstable types or under the influence of hallucination-inducing substances. Religious beliefs are also cited as the source of angelic abduction delusions, though some commentators argue that it might be more accurate to characterize the phenomenon as a type of modern-day folk myth (like the historic belief in Martians).

While some experts contend the field is rife with kooks and pseudoscience, there is little doubt that many apparently sincere persons report angelic abductions they believe are utterly genuine. Stigma and self-doubt may be obstacles to more widespread study.

Some abduction reports are quite detailed. The "terror abduction" experience is reported mainly in the USA, while in the rest of the world, particularly France, the encounters are said to be largely benevolent. An entire subculture has developed around the subject, with prayer groups and a detailed mythos explaining the reasons for abductions. Various angels (cherubim, seraphim, "Archangels" and so on) are said to have specific roles, origins, and motivations. Abduction claimants do not always attempt to explain the phenomenon, but others take independent research upon themselves, and explain the lack of greater awareness of angelic abduction as the result of either governmental or humanistic interest in a cover-up.

Possibilities provoke serious thought:

Some non-contactees are intrigued by the entire phenomenon, but hesitate to make any definitive conclusions. One former Vice President of the United States asked "How can a person have any firmly held belief about this when it's so mysterious? The opinions of the true believers are hard to swallow; and the opinions of the die-hard skeptics are not based on reality either. There is some middle ground. It's clear that this is some sort of powerful subjective experience. But I do not know what the objective reality is. It's as if the evidence leads us in both directions." Similarly, a former Harvard president concluded, "The furthest you can go at this point is to say there's an authentic mystery here. And that is, I think, as far as anyone ought to go."

Putting aside the question of whether abduction reports are literally and objectively "real", literature professor Terry Matheson argues that their popularity and their intriguing appeal is easily understood. Tales of abduction "are intrinsically absorbing; it is hard to imagine a more vivid description of human powerlessness." After experiencing the frisson of delightful terror one may feel from reading the Holy Bible or watching *The Passion of the Christ*, Matheson notes that people "can return to the safe world of their homes, secure in the knowledge that the phenomenon in question cannot follow. But as the contact myth has stated from the outset, there is no avoiding a guardian angel."

Matheson writes that when compared to the ancient reports, modern accounts are distinguished by their "relative sophistication and subtlety, which enable them to enjoy an immediately more favorable reception from the public."

Different cases vary in detail (sometimes significantly), but there is a broad, fairly consistent sequence and description of events which make up the typical "close encounter of the angelic kind".

The rest of the world is different:

There are however cultural differences in perception of these reported incidents. Although in North America, guardian angels are the most commonly blamed in these incidents, in Eastern Europe and other parts of the world, they are as often perceived to be demonic in origin.

The individual(s) concerned are often traveling by automobile at the time of the incident, usually at night or in the early morning hours, and usually in a rural or sparsely populated area. An angel will be seen ahead (sometimes on the road), and the driver will either deliberately stop to investigate, or the car will stop due to apparent mechanical failure. Interference is also common, such as a car radio producing static or behaving abnormally. On the occasions when they have been present, animals such as dogs usually also display a heightened fear response.

Upon exiting the vehicle, the driver and passenger(s) typically experience a blank period and amnesia, after which they find themselves again standing in front of their car. They very often do not consciously remember the experience. In some older cases, abductees occasionally reported symptoms consistent with nuclear radiation sickness.

As noted above, the so-called cherubim are most popularly associated with abduction reports, outpacing guardian angels and demons. Again, however, this seems to be a North American paradigm best-known since the 1980s and the appearance of smoking cherubim on the cover of a Van Halen album.

Actual proof?

Dr. Dan D. Derriere writes, "In many of these accounts, there is independent confirmation of missing time--emotionally stable people arriving hours late after long or short automobile journeys. For example, my research assistant and I regularly encounter angels near the Motel 6 close by campus. As my colleagues and family members can attest, we are consistently unable to account for approximately two hours of time most Tuesday afternoons."

Most intriguing are recently declassified documents demonstrating decades of government investigation into angelic phenomenon. Moreover, government complicity in suppressing legitimate angelic research is indisputable. For unknown reasons, the Air Force focused a great deal of attention in the Los Angeles area in 1952. Could this be the rumored Great Angel Manifestation? Is it possible that the government recovered a live angel?

More recently, some in the angelical community have suggested that the government has used holy technology to advance U.S. goals. How else to explain Stealth aircraft, iPods, or those cool new computerized voting booths? Some have even suggested that it is not too far a leap to believe that angels sit in on meetings at the highest levels of American government and business. Members of the White House and Capitol may even have been abducted by angels and now possess revelations pertinent to their decision-making.

In This Time Of Pestilence And Domination

Instead of chanting in Martin Luther King park
I climbed my thick tired bicycle
Intending to breathe deep and clear
In this age of pestilence and domination

Down to the canal I rode
And turned onto that path
Of so many free rides

Coming face to face with the SWAT team
Under the bridge

Hours before the tear gas
And rubber bullets and pepper spray

And burning police cars

And I pedaled through confusion
Contemplating their multi-colored camo
And multi-colored faces
Not knowing who to tell

But we all ought to know
The SWAT team waits under the bridge

THE PAINTED LADY
ON HALLOWEEN

"Oh, look, honey, she's dressed as a witch!" reassured the mother as her child gripped her hand tightly.

Judith smiled at the little girl, "You must be one of those superheroes from the movies. You look so much bigger on the screen." Then, she cackled at her own joke.

Wee Wonder Woman gritted her teeth, held out her plastic pumpkin and announced, "Trick or treat!"

"Well, of course, dearie," responded Judith. "I choose treat and I hope you do, too." She dropped a packet of Smarties into the bucket. Ignoring the recipient's disappointment, Judith closed the door.

She gave credit to any child who approached her Gothic painted lady, all orange, white and black. The facade lured some, but the rest had screwed up their courage.

Pausing before the mirror over the umbrella stand, Judith scratched her crooked nose. She smiled at her reflection. "You match your house; you're both painted ladies tonight," said the clerk down the street when she stopped in the convenience store for candy. The daring little rascals who looked so sad about sweet and sour tablets had no idea the slimness of the selection when you bought candy right before sunset on October 31.

Everything about the holiday was an afterthought for Judith. Really on a roll, she grinned. The whole night would be about afterthoughts, wouldn't it?

The doorbell rang.

Judith went to her small cauldron and grabbed a candy for this caller. The iron kettle had been a chore to drag up from the basement, but tradition weighed heavily on Judith. She would ask Frank or Tony to put it away later. Opening the front door slowly, Judith revealed herself.

Older or at least taller, who could tell underneath the sheet? They had cut holes large enough for the wide-eyed look given to Judith when she appeared. The tall hat and black dress could be a lot. Add on the bulbous nose, the makeup and the purple, grey hair...

The child held his ground and extended a paper bag.

"Yes?" Judith made her voice sing and demand all at once.

When no response came, she gave the child a noticeable once over. He wore sneakers and white socks.

"Well?" Judith prepared to rap the boy on the forehead with her knuckles.

"Happy Halloween?" he asked.

Judith puckered her lips. "Let me see your legs," Judith growled.

The boy's eyes expanded further, but he freed one hand from the bag and pulled the sheet upward.

"Stop! That's enough. This isn't that sort of thing," she grinned and dropped the candy in his bag.

With a great exhalation, he gripped the bag to his chest and dashed off her porch.

Judith saw a gaggle approaching, herded toward her house by their parents. She could not cope with so many at once, so she stepped inside, slammed the door, and turned off the porch light. Undeterred, they mounted her wooden steps like cattle and pounded her beautiful mahogany door.

"Go away!" shouted Judith. "I'm all out of candy!"

The children complained, but the adults laughed. They had probably come to Judith's house as trick-or-treaters themselves. They had tasted the rarity of seeing the old witch, so they tried every year to recreate the same frisson in their offspring.

Once the hubbub moved down the street, Judith retreated to her kitchen. She went into her small backyard, bordered by an old wooden fence and thorny bushes. Prying eyes struggled to spy on her private life. Her largest cauldron boiled on the grill. She really should have used the firepit, but she wanted to finish off the old bag of charcoal. Besides, the men might want to grill burgers later.

Smiling to herself, Judith approached the bat house nailed to the shed. Jenny had painted it pink and green before they hung it. That was before the pediatric cancer had taken her daughter and the colors had faded from the wood.

"In autumn, we need eye of newt, wing of bat and sparrow's heart to save a father from falling apart," she announced to no one in particular.

Two Easters after Jenny passed, the librarian in town had pointed Judith toward an old witch more than a state away. For mothers, the woman used eggs and rabbit organs and chocolate. Judith stayed and studied witchcraft for three years.

Inside the little basket nailed to a nearby oak tree, Judith found her pack of menthol cigarettes. The mint gentled the smoke, which mattered. She kept an old Harley Davidson lighter with the pack and used it to light one stick from the Natural American Spirit Dark Green pack. Working up to a deep inhale, she replaced the tools in their plastic baggie and returned it to the basket.

Judith bent over and exhaled smoke into the bat house. Then, she repeated twice, standing upright to inhale each time.

Reaching into the narrow aperture, Judith extracted a sedated bat. Her palm hugged the creature with gratitude. As she walked back to her patio, she steeled herself for the next step. After grabbing her cleaver, she placed the bat on a block of wood and halved it with one smooth swing after pulling her gripping hand out of the way. A little blood pooled as she removed the wings and hung them to drain. When she had added the rest to her compost, she washed the wings and placed them in her large boiling cauldron. Then she rinsed her chopping block with the hose.

The doorbell interrupted. A little girl dressed as a princess awaited in a charming pose. She, at least, smiled gratefully for the Smarties.

When Judith returned to the backyard, she headed for the terrarium on the side of the patio. "If only they made eye patches for newts," she said. "This would be much easier." She grabbed three different lizards before finding one still possessing both eyes. Deftly, she extracted the left one with her plastic stirrer from the old diner downtown.

Stepping precisely, she balanced the eye in the tiny spoon and reached the cauldron. She had not always made it on the first try and she envisioned a few tiny eyeballs deteriorating where the grass met her patio. Contemplating the boiling mixture, Judith always wondered at the ratio—bat wings floated so much larger, and the newt eye had already dissolved.

Judith retrieved her carefully labelled potion cup from the nearby table and half filled it with the mixture from the cauldron. Before going inside, she stopped to pop heads off her flowers and fill a small bowl with them. Their enchanting aroma went far to dissipate the stink from her potion cup.

Back inside, Judith set the teakettle to boil. Then she settled by the window to wait. The standard trick-or-treaters who braved her doorstep arrived before sunset. They had built their courage since breakfast and saw no need to wait any longer than the official start time declared by the town. She knew all about little children and the fears of parents. As the sun skittered out of sight and the moon shone brighter, Judith wished them all well.

The kettle whistled and she prepared the tea with the flower parts. On special occasions like this, she used her favorite cosy, designed like a warm sweater requiring her to button up the pot.

The gate way out back of the house banged. She watched Frank Morton walk across the grass, stepping carefully on her paving stones. All of the fathers preferred to stay on the path and avoid her bat house and terrarium and kettle and all the signals they had wandered somewhere outside their normal experience.

Tony Santino arrived next. Frank waited on the edge of the patio for him. Together they knocked on the kitchen door. Judith motioned them inside.

"I'm glad you're here," she greeted.

As he had for three years now, Tony admired the buttons on the teapot. He smiled at the sight and pushed the grin away almost as quickly. "Is it the usual?"

Judith smiled gently, "Absolutely. If you're still coming around, then I assume you like and need a nice herbal tea."

"For sure. Better than store bought," Frank said and took from beside the sink his usual mug, the one with the two cartoon characters in the pumpkin patch. "I'm hoping this is my last year."

Judith patted his hand and then filled his cup. "Me too," she encouraged.

They all looked up when Dave Mitchell walked in without knocking. He closed the door with both hands and surveyed the table. "I brought cookies." He presented a bakery box and laid it on the table. Then he adjusted it, so the edges ran in parallel to the table sides.

"You didn't have to," said Judith. Dave was their newest father, but she did not want to call attention to it.

Dave pointed at the extra chair, "Are we expecting someone? The cookies won't divide evenly."

"We'll make it work," reassured Judith.

Sensing someone approaching before the doorbell rang, Judith excused herself. She checked in the mirror. Instead of candy, she picked up her potion cup. Before opening the door, she said, "With respect, I fulfill my place in the community of all life."

Another ghost stood on the porch, covered in a mediocre costume, a sheet with black circles for eyes. The edges ended above tripping range at least. The child's father stood a few feet back and held a paper bag. He shifted from side to side.

"Look at you, dearie." Pursing her lips, Judith crouched down before the child. "You have a bit of a glow, did you know? You're the father? Do you see it on her, too?"

The man blew air out heavily before speaking. "Actually, it's a boy." He had not shaved in a week, and he looked as though he had dressed in a hurry. He had done up his jacket wrong and his socks did not match, not even close. "He's my son," he said this as though he needed convincing. "I made the costume in a hurry."

Judith reached out to the ghost and stroked his silken silver aura. Tiny stars stayed on her hand, glistened, and faded away. "What brings you here tonight?"

The man tilted his head at the unexpected question. "It's Halloween. We're trick-or-treating."

"Your son, have you taken him out every year?"

"Since he was two...," the man studied the empty lot next door before adding, "and not last year."

Judith nodded. "I understand." She turned back to the child. "Do you have a name, little man?"

After a pause, the man answered, "He's Georgie."

"How about you, sir?" asked Judith.

"I'm Randall. We used to live over on Cayuga." Randall's face twisted with the effort at maintaining his control. "I've been in the hotel by the highway for a few months. It's not bad, but Georgie always trick-or-treated here, and I wanted what he wanted."

The mute child bobbed impatiently.

Randall looked at the ground. "We never stopped at your house before. We'd heard things."

"It's all right. You're here now." Judith stared at him until he met her gaze. "Do you remember the feeling when you rip a bandage off a hairy spot on your skin? This is going to hurt a lot worse."

"What?"

Judith rapidly produced the potion cup from out of sight and broke its surface with her fingers. She sprinkled the mixture on the child. The black circles on the sheet concentrated on her every movement as she continued to administer the tonic. No words, no gesture objected.

"What are you doing?"In the weeks after Halloween and Easter, Judith often wondered if she should find a balm for this moment. Her teacher had none, so Judith did not. This was a ceremony of silence.

The child twinkled. The sheet condensed.

As it lowered slowly to the ground, Randall caught the nearest corner. Falling to his knees, his mouth moved, but no sound came. His wet eyes glared at her but found no solace in her placid expression. At the extreme end of his tether, Randall drew himself back to the present by pulling the sheet into a bundle against his chest.

Only then did Judith rise. With the gentlest of touches, she helped Randall to his feet. "Why don't you come inside?"

He found his voice before stepping forward, "I should go." Still, he let her lead him over the threshold and down the hall. Only in the doorway to the kitchen did she leave his side. "This is Randall. He's thinking about having a cup of tea."

The three men at the table gave Randall the once over. "Welcome," greeted Frank. "We understand."

"Have a seat," said Tony. "We can be here awhile, sometimes until sunrise." He pushed out the empty chair from under the table.

Randall nodded. He kept a tight grip on the sheet bundle but took a seat.

Dave said, "Look, I'm just going to say it. I didn't know you were coming, so there might not be enough cookies for everyone to have three."

Judith lifted the tea pot, "Chamomile tea?"

Does James Joyce Play Dice With the Universe?

Solange and Prestige celebrated their anniversary
With an Indian takeaway
Followed by a fantastic flourish before the convection oven
Culminating in subsequent exultant evacuations.

Only people of a certain age and confusion can appreciate
The pleasant surprise of survival
Commemorated by the foremost
Or the unexpected accomplishment of a little death
And a contribution to the universal midden.

ANY OTHER PERSON

She discovered she had turned into the wrong person.

Tamsin motioned to her lady in waiting and ordered her to bring the mirror from her bedchamber. "Don't look at me like that. Get one of the pageboys to help you if you can't handle a simple task."

While she waited, Tamsin listened to the knights continue their endless debating with her husband. She hated the king for his indecisiveness and pandering.

Across the oversized table dominating the throne room, Tamsin watched her attendant struggle with the floor length mirror along the walls. The young woman had chosen a new page to carry the other end.

Eventually, they placed the gold-framed looking glass beside Tamsin.

"Bring it closer, within arm's reach."

She admired the biceps on the burly lad. When she arrived in the kingdom, Tamsin found herself in the middle of an affair with one of the knights, who proved inattentive and dull. She sampled a quarter of the round table and a similar number of pages before seeing the futility. They were either drunk or rushed.

Tamsin gave the room a final survey and found it unchanged from her arrival. She licked the tip of her finger. She winked at the page who looked terrified. Then, she traced her reflection with her moist index finger.

***

She discovered she had turned into the wrong person.

"Excuse me? Are you going to give me the rest of my change or not?"

Tamsin pulled back from her abyss and refocused on the customer in front of her. "Yes, sorry. Three, four, five dollars." She gave the man in the Blink 182 shirt a professional nod and looked to the girl behind him.

"A pack of Marlboros," demanded the adolescent.

"I don't think you're old enough."

"They're for my mom."

Tamsin considered the four impatient people behind the girl and reached up for the pack.

"Could you make it a carton?" The girl smirked.

"No."

"Fine."

Six customers later, Tamsin saw her opportunity and made a dash for the restroom. Inside, she stood before the mirror, licked her finger, and...

***

Tamsin heard the librarian approach. She looked over the top of the study carousel.

"You can't keep staying in the library," said Cynthia.

They had been roommates their first two years at university, only ending when Tamsin moved off campus to live in her boyfriend's studio apartment. Tamsin did not want to get into a whole thing, so she kept her voice flat and unequivocal.

"I have a big project due Monday first thing. It's not like I'm the only person that ever gets locked in."

"You are the only person we've locked in for five nights running."

"Give me until Monday to sort something out. I need this."

Cynthia made the dramatic sigh she had perfected their freshman year and nodded.

Tamsin waited for the dimming of the overhead lights before taking the mirror out of her backpack. She touched up the concealer around the bruise on her face. She licked the tip of her index finger.

***

She discovered she had turned into the wrong people: a girl chatting with a hookah-smoking caterpillar; a pregnant gunfighter; a suburban soccer mom; a tomb raider; an unexpected guest.

***

She discovered she had turned into the wrong person.

The stench of drunken pirates hit Tamsin first. Men littered the deck of the sloop *William*. Somewhere in that mass, she would find her lover, Captain "Calico Jack" Rackham. Mary Read stood beside her, the pair being the sober exceptions. Tamsin followed Mary's eyes out to sea and watched an English privateer draw closer. They both drew their pistols.

"We are doomed," said Mary.

"They are bound to find us out."

"Damn Jack Rackham."

"I'm pregnant," hissed Tamsin.

"So am I."

"Damn Jack Rackham."

Mary shifted her pistol and took her friend's hand. As the first cannonball flew overhead, Tamsin lost her nerve.

"Does Jack still have that mirror in his cabin?"

***

Tamsin shifted books about in her carousel until she located her mobile.

"Cynthia, I'm sorry for calling so late, but you were right. I don't want to spend another night or even minute here. Can you come and let me out? And maybe I can stay at your place?"

Laurel's Torment or The Schadenfreude Villanelle

Schadenfreude was always near to Stanley
It was all so desultory and banal
But he could never forget Ollie

That morning, Laurel was shocked by the comedy
But still he remembered the protocol
Schadenfreude was always near to Stanley

Later, Laurel was spooked to a degree
Their act seemed repetitive, all in all
But he could never forget Ollie

He distracted Stan with physicality

Said it was time to work in a pratfall
Schadenfreude was always near to Stanley

Oliver took a leap most gracefully
Hardy flew high like a toxic theory
But Stan could never forgive Ollie

Laurel nosedived- O vengeful gravity
Stan's mind echoed dangerously eerie
Schadenfreude was always near to Stanley
For he could never forgive Ollie

Louis Bowel And The Non-Writing Movement

"He writes he writes he writes and his paper remains pure and white." So wrote Gertrude Stein in **The Lost Notebooks of Alice B. Toklas** in which she inferred the thoughts of her confidante, Alice B. Toklas, via osmosis. Of course, Stein was writing about one of the least read and most unpublished authors of our time, Louis Bowel. He would have it no other way. Countless authors have suffered through an extended Bowel Movement, brought on by deleterious behavior, but few have been as grateful for the experience as the namesake of the Non-Writing Movement.

So many authors, adequate to mediocre, have struggled with the pen and paper, but few have come by that struggle as innately as Louis Bowel. (Pronounced with the emphasis on the second syllable. "It has been said properly when it sounds

like you've knocked the wind out of a terrier in mid-bark."
—Louis Bowel in **Authors and Their Movements: a Turgid Study**.) Rare is the scholar who has reviewed Bowel's oeuvre and is not grateful for its brevity.

Louis Bowel first came to prominence on the Right Bank in Paris where he often sat watching the expatriate Americans picnic across the Seine. He would arrive shortly after sunrise and begin building a tidy pile of small pebbles. As the Americans arrived, Bowel would wait patiently while they unpacked their baskets and spread their blankets for a pleasant repast by the river. As the first bite was taken, the Americans found themselves bombarded by a storm of stones.

Bowel kept to this routine until his famous encounter with Hemingway. Refusing to retreat in the face of Bowel's barrage, Hemingway, filled with rage and slightly bruised, plunged into the Seine and swam across the river toward Bowel. Not being a fool, Bowel was long gone by the time Hemingway arrived. Neither one ever had a kind word for the other. "Bowel had no output," wrote Hemingway in **A Moveable Feast**. "He smelled like a donkey," countered Bowel.

Bowel spent the succeeding years writing little of note. He supported himself with stints in a German cabaret show and in a Paris jazz club, doing little for his reputation as an author. On the other hand, Bowel established himself as a tuba player of some repute. Only when Gertrude Stein invited him to her apartment for a recital did Bowel exhibit the first signs of renewed interest in writing. Apparently inspired by a recitation given by Stein, Bowel went home and wrote his great manifesto, *Why Bother*.

Few people have been able to read *Why Bother* and not feel the full pressure of a Bowel driven to distraction. He pounds away again and again, driving home the one great inspiration of his life-- apathy. This was a man who had nothing to offer and wanted everyone to know it. Scholars have long been disturbed by the lack of a question mark at the end of Bowel's title. Professor Ludwig Van Buren, Heidelberg University, deemed it "a damn foolish thing to worry about," while Professor Frank Happenstance, Mishkatoolah University, wrote "the work is not improved by the omission." Ultimately, this would be the only work Bowel would publish in his lifetime. His notebooks, discovered posthumously, were initially deemed illegible, but have been recently published by the University of Chicago Press as **A Hundred Monkeys Pounding on Typewriters (And We Mean No Insult to the Monkeys)**, ed. F. Happenstance.

World War II arrived, leaving no marks or fissures on Bowel who remained in Vichy France. In later years, he would claim to have considered joining the resistance. Even this small gesture allowed him to maintain the level of apathy to which he had grown accustomed and Bowel spent the war years ignored by the Nazis.

Why Bother served as a powerful inspiration to legions of graduate students after it first came to prominence in the late Forties. At that time, Evelyn Waugh wrote, "For a while there, it seemed like the only new work was being produced in newspapers and they were almost impossible to come by." No published author willingly associated with Bowel, perhaps fearful of falling under the seductive spell of his tuba and the passionate melancholy of his message. However, a slow procession of young Americans traveled across the Atlantic Ocean to study at the feet of the master.

Many scholars have attempted to capture the inner reality of *Why Bother* and have failed. Let me be another. Bowel began with the conclusion that no person relies so heavily on the power of language as an author. Authors collect language, plowing through it like a dung beetle through a rubbish heap. Each word, perhaps each syllable, maybe even every letter, has a distinct essence that the author channels. The true author uses only the most powerful words and the ageless giants require the fewest words to express their meaning. In fact, a true literary genius has found the purest expression and should feel no need to put it down on paper. When judging an author's collected writings, the reader's opinion should be based upon the slimness of that output. The critic should dispense with actual reading. Rather, a scale ought to be sufficient. Bowel concluded that the true author should merely have to identify himself as an author. If he has no actual output, then so be it.

The struggle for the literary genius is to find some way to occupy his time. A great author is therefore found in sidewalk cafes, drinking coffee and smoking cigarettes. He should stare off into space and order so little that the waiters grow annoyed. Bowel indicated in his final paragraph that the appropriate behavior of a literary aficionado was not to buy books by favored authors, but rather to purchase pastry, coffee, and cigarettes for those fine authors sitting at sidewalk cafes throughout Paris, particularly on Rue Jardin in the late morning.

Naturally, none of Bowel's hangers-on went on to write a single word of note, bringing the Non-Writing Movement to full flower. The Fifties were a time of great joy for Bowel. Willing to pay for his meals and listen to his frequent soliloquys, disciples surrounded Bowel. "He seemed genuinely disinterested in anyone else," says Eugene Bevaqua, one of Bowel's followers at the time and currently working on his doctoral thesis. "I remember so many nights sitting around waiting for something to happen."

Unfortunately for Bowel, his downfall came suddenly and swiftly, for a Judas resided in the ranks of his collegiate admirers. Young Beltham Barium II revealed Bowel as a charlatan. Barium's father owned a string of chalk mines in the American southwest and Beltham was due to inherit a large organized labor problem sometime in the near future. Louis Bowel welcomed the young Barium with open arms, recognizing in Beltham someone who could afford to buy a great deal of pastry.

Barium, like so many of his generation, was infatuated with *Why Bother*. He later described it as something he could wave in his father's face whenever discussion of finishing college arose. It was only after the elder Barium cut off his allowance that young Beltham considered the implications of *Why Bother*. Unlike anyone before him, Beltham Barium II gave serious thought to its content as a statement, rather than as an excuse. He brought all the force of a freshman logic course to bear in his own analysis and decided to transcribe his conclusions. He accused Bowel of self-contradiction since he had actually bothered to write down his denial of the value of writing.

The attack came out of nowhere as far as Bowel was concerned. He was constricted, unable to respond in kind because any written response would be viewed as a betrayal by his followers. He declared that reading was just as bad as writing, but his followers could not help but notice that Barium had been offered a choice of professorships at various prestigious universities based upon his critique of Bowel.

The words began to flow and Bowel became a hot topic in the literary establishment. Bowel himself gave a semester of lectures at Harvard in the spring of 1959, consisting of a series of improvisations on the tuba interrupted by long breaks for smoking. Unfortunately, this time proved to be a last burst of fame before oblivion for Bowel. None of his followers who had moved into the academic environment felt any need to produce scholarly work once they attained tenure. By 1961, Louis Bowel had been forgotten and authors were writing more words than anyone cared to read.

By the end of the century, Louis Bowel no longer lectured, but he continued not to write. He gave up the tuba in 1963, when he realized that he "despised the sound of the thing." Late in life, he received few visitors in his small apartment in Paris and those that did visit were treated rudely. He seemed comfortable with his legacy of apathy, although he admitted that he would have done one thing differently. "I would've fought Hemingway on the banks of the Seine. That story'd be worth a lot of free dinners."

Not Felt

I buried my heart in the garden.
This morning I unearthed
One and one half harts.
Oh deer.
I've reduced my life
To a joke.
Not a good one, but still...
I did bury my heart.

In The Eighties When Preston Got Sick And Sophie Died

Coughing with yellowed eyes and drooping skin, Preston looked like he'd been up half the night. "I want to write something." He filled the kitchen doorway with the comforter clutched around his body. He dragged half the blanket along behind him and settled into one of our godawful chairs. I don't know how it supported him and the blanket without racing away from beneath him.

I was a little hurt. "What do you want to write about?"

"I need to write about Sophie..."

"You're the talker. I'm the writer. You talk and I'll write it down." He had been sick for almost a month and a half. "You look like shit. And you smell like it too. Maybe you could take a shower today?"

Preston smiled. "Yea, I ran into Derek in the hallway and he turned kind of pale when I passed him."

Derek was pissed that I had let Preston crash in my room for so long. Four of us had taken the house last fall and now there were seven of us living in it. Derek was the only one not sharing a bedroom. I don't know what Stacy or Frank did with their guests, but Preston sure as hell hadn't offered anything toward my rent. He still had his apartment over in Somerville anyway. He'd just been crashing with me since he'd gotten sick at Sophie's potluck memorial dinner.

"You heard from anybody else?" Preston asked the same question every morning. He wasn't the only one sick after the potluck and some of their diseases lingered too.

I shrugged in response as I had every morning. I was fine, so I knew he had just had bad luck. "You want some hot tea or something?"

Preston nodded. "You know I really loved Sophie."

***

I always felt a little weird about how much Preston loved Sophie. She was my dog after all. But she seemed to prefer him. Sophie was how we met. Preston had family near that house in Arlington and I ran into him a couple times while walking Sophie. I liked this little cemetery in the center of town. It dated back to Revolutionary times, like just about everything else around Boston, but it was right in my neighborhood. I took Sophie there and Preston apparently dug spending time with the long dead when he needed a break from his family.

We talked and hung out some. He was even more into the Celtics than me, though McHale was his guy, while I knew the world revolved around Bird. We must have watched every game together that season, weeping at the end- fucking Lakers.

The absolute worst thing about that loss was it happened on the same day of Sophie's vet appointment- fucking vets. She had a tumor and they could operate, but it wasn't going to change much other than break my bank account. My heart would break anyway.

The thing about dogs and cancer is that it happens fast. Or maybe we only find out when it's so late. Really, I only know it happened fast with Sophie. She stopped eating a month later and a couple days after she stopped moving from her spot in the kitchen. Derek was the only roommate to give me shit about it, but Preston had a word with him. By that time, Preston stopped by each day for a few hours. In the end, he sat on that tiled floor with me and Sophie for a few hours every evening. She'd dig her tan and gray snout into my belly, turning my shirt dark with snot and mist. I missed enough work that I worried about making rent, especially when I caught a cold. We tried to have Sophie share our beer in case it would help, but she wouldn't eat or drink anything anymore. We sat with Sophie wheezing and me sneezing.

On the last night, Preston went home and I fell asleep beside Sophie on the floor. She was big enough to be a good pillow for me, but I was afraid to put any weight on her.. I woke to shuddering. That was it- three shakes and she was gone.

I called Preston and he had to catch a cab because his car was a piece of shit. I hadn't the willpower to do anything anymore. Preston cast a long shadow in the kitchen when he arrived. "What are you going to do now?"

"I don't know." I started crying and making noises that I didn't know I could make.

After I ran down a bit, Preston went to the sink, soaked a towel in cold water, and handed it to me. "Wipe your face. You know, we ought to bury her." He crouched down beside Sophie and me. "Don't you think?" He had this way of talking where he tilted his head back and you looked right up his nostrils. I wondered if I looked hard enough whether I might see his thoughts forming.

I nodded my agreement without fully thinking through the implications. The house didn't have much of a yard, so I had no idea what Preston might be planning. Moreover, Preston thought we ought to have a wake. He got on the phone. I couldn't raise myself off the floor or even move Sophie's fore paws off my thigh.

"Are you ready?" Preston was back in my face, dragging a cardboard box from somewhere.

I wiped my face with the back of my hand while Preston slid Sophie off me. She weighed less than I expected. He carried the box. I could not have taken those first steps with her. The setting sun blinded us as we headed west toward the cemetery. I demanded the box from Preston. Bordered by main streets, we had to cross five lanes of traffic to get to the stone wall marking the edge of the old burial ground. I expected a police car to screech to a halt beside us and demand an explanation as well as a look inside the box. The authorities did not approve of us hanging out anywhere.

The irregular stone wall had collapsed in places. The crypts were in no better condition, some askew enough to be open. Preston had always talked about exploring one of them and he led me straight for the corner out of sight of the street. I could see the dark maw ahead and I dragged my feet though I didn't stop. As we grew closer, I imagined heaving the box through the hole and running back to the house in a fit of hysteria.

Except Preston paused about eight feet away from the opening, which was too far for me to throw Sophie. "This one still has steps." I knew what he meant, but only managed a vision of us stumbling down the stairs in a tangle of limbs and embarrassment. "We can try to close the door after we leave her." Preston stood between me and the crypt, haloed by the setting sun, reaching out for poor, dead Sophie. I will never forget Sophie on that kitchen floor or Preston in that last glow of an unbidden day. Maybe that's not how they want to be remembered.

I think we helped each other down into the hole. As we went deeper, it smelled more and more of wet and of green. We crouched and moved slowly in the darkness. I don't really know what touched us along the walls, as close as they were, but it definitely felt like old death. Even in the coolness, sweat broke out all over me.

"Are you frightened?" asked Preston. "Don't you see that this is a good place down here? Sophie will be all right here." He began lowering the box and I went down with him onto that soft, moist blackness. "Goodbye, Sophie. You were a good dog."

I had not felt the tears start, but they came in a torrent. "Best dog ever," I screeched from somewhere deep inside that I had not wanted touched. The mud seeped into my knees.

I followed Preston to the surface and we tried to close the crypt door, but only managed to move it an inch before we had embedded it even deeper in the ground. Preston walked away, but I couldn't stand. I tore handfuls of blooming dandelions from the ground cover and tossed them into the darkness of the hole until I felt a hand on my shoulder. Preston had come back for me. My runny nose worsened as we stumbled back to the house.

The next morning, I woke early and made the chili for the potluck. I didn't know half the people Preston had invited. I spent most of the night watching him from the easy chair where I planted my ass. People took turns comforting me until only Preston remained. He slept on the sofa beside the easy chair and woke up the next morning with his damned cough. And for many more mornings.

***

"So, what do you want to write about Sophie?"

"I don't know. You write it."

I looked at him wondering what this was about. He stared out the kitchen window, so I bent over the pad of paper.

Before I could scratch the first letter, he grabbed my hand. "Just make sure they know she had some good days and some bad days. She was a good dog."

"Best dog ever," I said.

DRAFT DAY

I seek an alternative
To kill or be killed
The worms in the foxhole
Care not whom they devour
Like the commander
Bathing in his gold tub in his ivory tower
The blood slides down the porcelain
Tracing an ellipsis
That defies the gravity

The Meeting Of All Meetings

"Karl Marx-- one of the greatest conspiracy theorists the world has ever seen." Rich looked around the room, waiting for a gasp. When none came, he continued, "Think about it. He looked at a bunch of past events and saw all these connections. He applied a retrospective view to a selected group and observed a pattern."

Curtis raised both his hands and declared, "Hold it. Last month, you praised Ayn Rand's insight. Before that, some guy named Leopold von Ranke."

"No, I said Ranke had some good ideas. My talk was about obfuscation. He said looking for patterns was a fool's game, but he really liked good evidence."

Hannah nodded, "Ranke was the guy who wanted primary sources. Right?"

Marta shook her head, "No, I think you have it wrong. He was the guy who just made things up to please everybody."

Hannah answered, "You're thinking of Tacitus, the Roman who slandered the dead. Rich talked about them both three months ago, the day of the Super Bowl party. You remember when Francis forgot to bring beer?"

Francis opened his eyes. "I didn't forget. I don't like beer so why would I buy it for you lot?" He always looked half-asleep until someone mentioned his name. More dramatic in seminars, the expression could still be effective in small groups.

Marta tapped her Apple Watch, "We need to be out of here by eight. The future marketers club have the room reserved then."

Rich clicked on his presentation, "If you'll let me continue, Marx wrote about whole populations..."

"Exactly, so how is it a conspiracy if everyone is involved?" demanded Curtis.

Francis rose to his feet, then considered his audience and sat back down. "I want to talk about something. I know I haven't taken my turn since we started meeting in person again."

"And you didn't come to any of the Zoom meetings," sniffed Marta.

Francis gave her his look that made you wish he would go back to being sleepy-eyed. "We held our first meeting during our freshman year, and we graduate in three weeks. In all our time together, have we ever found a real conspiracy?"

"Kennedy was killed by the CIA," stated Curtis.

"Agreed, but nothing current, right?"

"Area 51, David Icke, Bernie Madoff, Jeffrey Epstein," Hannah ticked each on her fingers.

Francis frowned with his entire face, "I thought we preferred secret conspiracies. If it's in the past or the investigation is sanctioned by the government, then it's not much of a conspiracy, is it?"

Rich shook his head, "But what else is there? Everybody's a conspiracy theorist now, what with QAnon and all the rest."

Francis ambled over to Rich's computer and typed.

"Oh, all right... go ahead," allowed Rich.

Francis talked over his shoulder at the other four, "When the university sent us home and we had to go to all our classes remotely, I got bored. I had to choose either my mom or my dad to stay with and I made the wrong choice. My dad took to wine hard which meant he slept about fourteen hours a day."

"The apple doesn't fall far from the tree," muttered Hannah.

"I heard you," responded Francis. "I don't drink, but I do like to sleep. Maybe you're right." He went back and sat down.

"I meant...."

Francis struck his half-awake pose.

"Come on," said Curtis. "Show what you have or admit you bullshitted."

Francis pointed at Rich's laptop.

"It's a Zoom meeting," said Rich.

"Join it," directed Francis.

They watched as the application took them to the waiting room until some unseen benefactor granted them admittance. The screen filled with tiny pictures of people.

Rich leaned in close and clicked through pages, "There must be hundreds of people in here. I didn't know you could do a Zoom this large."

"The number is closer to a thousand," said Francis.

"I'm going to stop scrolling," said Rich.

They all moved closer to the screen.

"What is this? They look like they're all talking at once." Hannah turned to find Francis had stepped back. He had always needed the most personal space.

"I started typing in meeting numbers at random," his voice fought a growing fright. "I think this is how the world is run now."

"What are you talking about?" Even Curtis sounded put off.

"Look, there are breakout rooms and people keep coming and going." Francis waved a finger at the monitor, as if he could comprehend it with an all-encompassing gesture. "I can't wrap my mind around it."

"Isn't that Biden?" asked Marta. "Mitch McConnell? Piers Morgan?"

"Isn't he talking to the leader of New Zealand? What's her name?" Rich had lost all interest in Karl Marx. "This is a meeting of meetings. Look, it's Kevin Bacon."

"Is it some sort of overarching master meeting of all Zoom meetings?" Hannah shook her head before anyone could argue with her. "Maybe you found an IT support loophole."

"The mother of all meetings," offered Curtis. "Stop scrolling! That's Xi Jinping!"

"How can you even tell who is talking to who?" asked Hannah.

"Why not ask them?" said Curtis. "We're in there with them, right?"

"Oh, shit," Hannah looked at Rich accusingly. "You don't have the camera on, do you? What about all the router hopping I spoke about two years ago. Do none of you listen to my presentations?"

"I can't access the campus library if I set my laptop up that way." Rich grabbed at the laptop and typed desperately.

"Where are you going?" demanded Curtis when he saw Francis heading for the door.

"It doesn't matter," said Francis, "I think it's too late."

The knock on the door sounded official.

The New England Chapter of Broken-Hearted Ghosts

The chairs remain stacked against the walls like cordwood.
The New England Chapter of Broken-Hearted Ghosts
meets here. Out of fear, the lights remain on all the
time. Hawthorne and Irving rotate the chairmanship.
The religious gather in cliques and bemoan their
purgatory. Unable to grasp the gavel,
the meeting can never be called to order. The
recent dead recant their lies and recriminations.
Among the former atheists, conversation
is muted. Many are lost in their own thoughts. The
specter of past meetings haunts the secretary's
minutes. This endless assembly. This embrace of smoke

ALSO BY KOJ BOOKS

Five Raging Hearts: Splatterpunk for the Soul

Three novellas and two short stories from the hearts of Craig Brownlie, Roxane Llanque, Mathew L. Reyes, Judith Sonnet, and Wile E. Young, with an introduction by Bitter Karella
<u>*And from Craig Brownlie:*</u>

Post Apocalyptic Policing With Frida Kahlo

<u>**Read all the Little Books of Pain:**</u>
#1 Hammer Nail Foot
#2 Thick As A Brick
#3 A Book Of Practical Monsters

<u>For YA, MG, and Young at Heart readers:</u>
Comic Book Summer

Trigger Warnings

The various poems throughout the book refer to war, bodily fluids, sex, abortion, existential fear, politics, protests, police actions, and ghosts.

Thick As A Brick: death of children and spouse; cosmic horror; child harm; hoarding.

The Circus Came To Town: COVID and associated topics; death of spouse; clowns.

Writing Home From A Great Remove: cremation; burning alive; slavery; slave trade; misogyny.

The Painted Lady At Halloween: death of children; witchcraft with associated harm to animals.

Any Other Person: abuse.

In The Eighties When Preston Got Sick And Sophie Died: death of a pet.

About The Author

Craig believes the Baby Taj Mahal (Itmad-ud-Daula) is more fun to visit than its more famous sibling across the Yamuna River. He thinks you ought to feel however you want about angels, hoarding, grief, and James Joyce. Even so, be careful out there because every path leads in two directions, at least. Also, being cryptic is not the same as being wise or intelligent.

Look for Craig's work in *Demons and Death Drops*, *No More Resolutions*, *Lovecraftiana*, *Sci-Fi Lampoon Magazine*, and *Unspeakable Horrors 3*. He contributes randomly to Uncomfortably Dark.

Visit Craig and sign up for his newsletter at
https://craigbrownlie.com/
Friend him on Facebook.
and Instagram.
Or talk to him at a convention.